YVES SAINT LAURENT
"Tribute to Wesselmann" dress
France, 1966

SONIA DELAUNAY
Fabric pattern
France, 1930s

YVES SAINT LAURENT
"Barbaresque" dress
France, 1958–59

PATRICK COX
Spectator shoe
England, 1990s

YVES SAINT LAURENT
"Mondrian" print
France, 1965

SALVATORE FERRAGAMO
Rainbow platform shoe
Italy, 1938

DE PINNA
Houndstooth check pattern
USA, 1885

ANDRÉ PERUGIA
Fish shoe for Georges Braque
France, 1951

BALLY
Pump
Switzerland, 1914

The illustrations in this book were made with pen and ink and watercolor.

Library of Congress Cataloging-in-Publication Data

Guarnaccia, Steven.
Cinderella : a fashionable tale / retold and illustrated by Steven Guarnaccia.
pages cm
Summary: Retells the classic fairy tale of the young servant girl who experiences
a magical night and finally finds her prince. Features illustrations of apparel
and accessories inspired by famous fashion designers.
ISBN 978-1-4197-0986-9
[1. Fairy tales. 2. Folklore.] I. Title.
PZ8.G94Ci 2013
398.2—dc23
[E]
2013006459

First Italian edition published by Maurizio Corraini srl in 2013
under the title *Cenerentola: Una favola alla moda.*

Printed and bound at Viadana (Mn), Italy
10 9 8 7 6 5 4 3 2 1

Abrams Books for Young Readers are available at special discounts when purchased in quantity for
premiums and promotions as well as fundraising or educational use. Special editions can also be
created to specification. For details, contact specialsales@abramsbooks.com or the address below.

ABRAMS
THE ART OF BOOKS SINCE 1949

115 West 18th Street
New York, NY 10011
www.abramsbooks.com

Cinderella
a fashionable tale

retold & illustrated by
Steven Guarnaccia

Abrams Books for Young Readers, New York

There once was a young girl who lived with her cruel stepmother and three stepsisters. Because she was always covered in ashes, her stepsisters teased her and called her Cinderella.

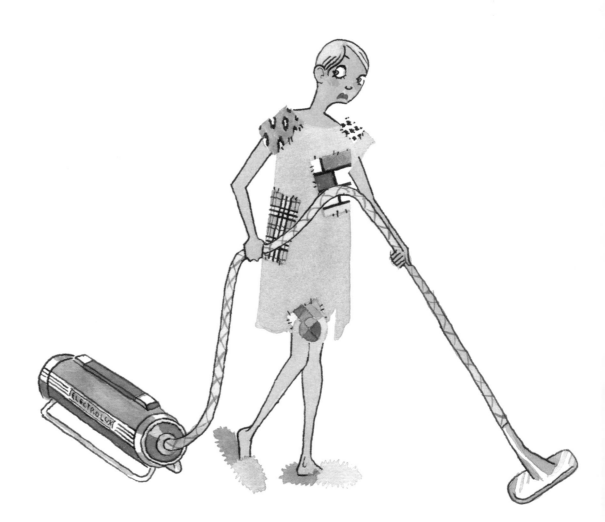

Her stepsisters would sit around eating cake while Cinderella washed the clothes, swept the floor, and did the dishes. While her stepsisters dressed in the finest clothes and slept in the softest beds, Cinderella dressed in rags and slept in a corner by the fireplace.

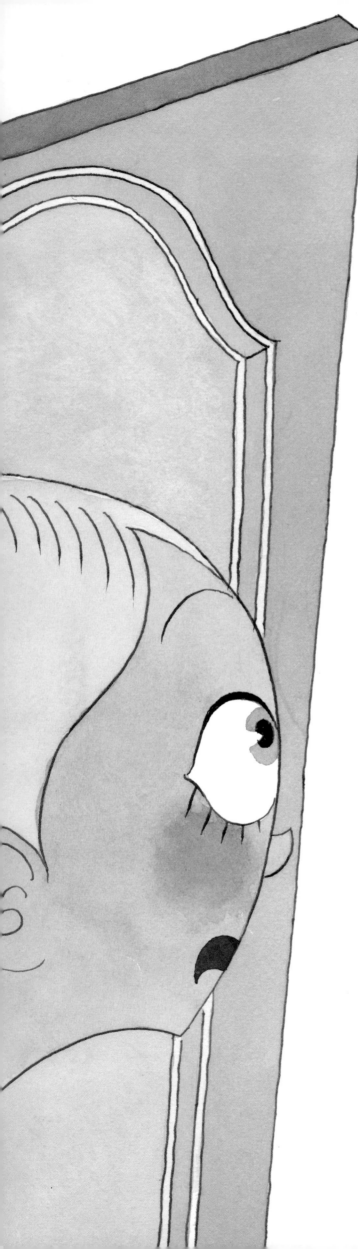

One day, the prince invited everyone in town to a ball. But Cinderella's stepmother wouldn't allow her to attend.

As the stepsisters chose their clothes for the ball, they laughed and said, "Can you imagine Cinderella at the ball in *her* clothes?"

On the night of the ball, Cinderella's stepmother and stepsisters went off in a coach, leaving Cinderella to cry alone in her corner by the fire.

When Cinderella's magical godfather heard her sobs,
he immediately appeared and offered to help her.

"Fetch me the biggest
pumpkin from the
garden," he said.

When she brought it to him, he zapped it once with his
wand . . . and it turned into a golden coach.

"Now fetch me a fat mouse from the cellar," said her godfather.

Cinderella did so, and she watched as he waved his wand over the mouse, turning it instantly into a coachman.

"Now", said her godfather, "for your clothes . . ."

He tapped Cinderella twice with his wand, and her torn and dirty rags became one beautiful gown after another. At last she chose one, and on her feet appeared a pair of crystal slippers.

Her godfather sent Cinderella off in the coach, saying, "Don't forget to leave the ball by midnight. One minute longer and everything — coach and driver, gown and shoes — will return to the way it was."

When
Cinderella
arrived at
the ball, the
guests all
stopped to
gaze at her,
assuming
she was a
beautiful
princess.

The prince spent the entire evening dancing with
Cinderella, never guessing that she was a poor servant girl.

As the clock struck midnight, Cinderella ran from the ballroom, losing one of her crystal slippers on the way.

When Cinderella arrived at the coach, it turned back into a pumpkin, the coachman turned back into a mouse, and she was once again dressed in rags.

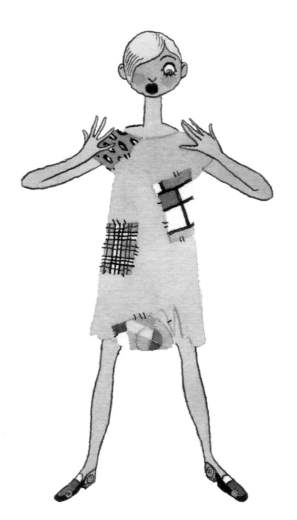

The prince tried to follow Cinderella out of the ball, but when he asked his footmen if they had seen a beautiful princess leave, they replied that no one had left but a poor servant girl.

When her stepsisters returned from the ball, they told Cinderella all about the mysterious princess and the crystal slipper she had left behind.

The next day, the prince issued a proclamation, stating that he would marry the owner of the crystal slipper. The prince's assistants went from house to house, trying the crystal slipper on the feet of every woman and girl in the land.

Cinderella's stepsisters tried on the crystal slipper, but it didn't fit any of them.

"Perhaps it will fit me," said Cinderella.

Her sisters said, "Of all the nerve!" and "Don't be ridiculous!".

When the prince's footman tried the shoe on Cinderella,
and it fit perfectly, the stepsisters' jaws dropped. When
Cinderella took the other crystal shoe out of her pocket
and slipped it on as well, her stepsisters nearly fainted.

The prince was delighted to find the rightful owner of the crystal slipper. He looked into Cinderella's eyes and at once recognized her as the beautiful princess he had danced with all evening at the ball. The prince immediately invited Cinderella to his castle, where they were married soon after.

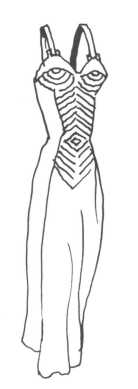

JEAN PAUL GAULTIER
"Pink Corset" dress
France, 2010

ELSA SCHIAPARELLI
(WITH SALVADOR DALÍ)
Shoe hat
France, 1937-38

PAUL POIRET
Party costume
France, 1911

KANSAI YAMAMOTO
Bodysuit designed for
David Bowie's Aladdin Sane tour
Japan, 1973

PAUL SMITH
Multistripe dressing gown
England, 2010

CHARLES JAMES
"Four-leaf clover" dress
USA, 1953